7%

© 2011 David Samuel Neuer. All rights reserved.
ISBN 978-1-257-76651-2

Cast of Characters

Jack:	solving the math problem of life
Mark:	studying to become a priest
Anna/Love:	Jack's poetry girlfriend
Jennifer/Death:	Mark's girlfriend in the Catholic Studies program
Mark's Dad:	Mark's father
Prof:	Theology professor
Class:	Theology class
Counselor:	meets with patients at the crisis residence
Monk:	guest of Theology class
Nurse:	helps out at the crisis residence
Priest:	Mark's priest
Sixties Hippie:	mental health patient (guy)
Suicidal Girl:	mental health patient (girl)

ACT I

Scene I

open mic night; bar

ANNA

Chaffed lips as the wind blows the smoke from my snowy face. A tale from a scarf whispers hollow tales of heavenly landscapes. Sparkling warmth coats the stomach lining of my ulcer, bred for painful reading of past events, dripping down the back of my throat like sweet candied thoughts, savoring bitter flavors on the palette of a chipped shoulder, wearing souls on her sleeve as she constructs humorous tangents.

MARK

Trapped. Pushing on the ceiling. Pushing on the walls. Stomping on the ground. Let me out of my skin. Alien, I do not belong in this body. Birth me again mother, in a different life in a different land, in an age and generation not of this time, to my place of solitude. Let me die in peace, not in swamps of fear and sweat. Cripple me once and for all.

JENNIFER

Grasping. Wishing to take hold of hope. Food be my console and comfort. Stand by my side as I lust in want, waiting. The barren land yearns and mourns waiting in pain crying rainstorms and floods. The eye of the hurricane foreshadows the quiet death.

JACK

I've studied math for quite some time now, and have been stuck on this one particular equation for what seems like an eternity. This integral problem stretches to infinity, and it's called my life. It is definitely solvable using Calculus. I set the parameters from hell to heaven, negative infinite to infinity. Haha, that's a joke, but honestly, I have studied most of the world's religions and I am still searching. Searching for some piece of truth. Oh, what is truth? If only truth were a number.

Scene II

in theology class, a prof writes 7% on a chalk board

PROF

Seven percent. Seven percent of atheists can get into Catholic heaven. There is a catch. They have to be actively searching for something.

Jack raises his hand

PROF

Yes, Jack.

JACK

Is that how Catholics accept Jews into heaven, since most Jews are atheists?

murmuring among the students

PROF

Your question does have some theological foundation. When Jacob wrestled God, God could not overpower him. He wrenches Jacobs hip. Jacob still does not let him go. He demands that God bless him. God tells him he shall be called Israel because he, "struggled with God and man and overcame." As Christians we too wrestle with God, which means we too are Israelites. I am getting slightly off topic. Just know that doubting God does not mean losing faith in God. We all wrestle with God.

to the audience

JACK

I had been struggling with faith my whole life. I was raised in a southern Bible belt church with a legalistic approach to faith. God was the eternal judge like Dostoevsky had written about in Brothers. I was the defendant on trial trying to get acquitted so I could get into heaven. Let me make a clarification, I struggled inside my faith. Once I got to college, it became an external struggle. It was like an advanced algebra problem where everything started out in parenthesis and got foiled. First-Out-Inner-Last. Everything got multiplied and there were all these positive and negative numbers and variables. Don't get me started on the variables.

enter Buddhist Monk

PROF
Today's class is dedicated to learning the OHM mantra.

MONK
Your mind is clear. Say it together now--OHM.

CLASS
OHM

MONK
Nothing exists in the world--OHM.

CLASS
OHM

MONK
The noises you hear do not exist.

student raises his hand

JACK
What if I hear the train going by in the distance? I hear it's whistles, and I hear the sounds of it rushing along the tracks...

MONK
All sounds should pass by like they do not exist. Now keep going.

CLASS
OHM...OHM...OHM

MONK
All the thoughts that enter your head pass on by like the breeze.

CLASS
OHM.

MONK
They blow on by.

CLASS
OHM.

MONK
Your eyes are closed.

CLASS
OHM

MONK
Now silence. Breath through your nose. You feel the breath from your nostrils exiting. The sounds and thoughts pass by like waves. Now what do you want to meditate upon?

JACK
Upon nothing teacher. I do not want any thoughts to plague my mind.

MONK
But what must you meditate upon?

JACK
I must focus on guidance. For my future is uncertain. It sits built upon sand and must be constructed upon sturdier ground.

MONK
Guidance is what you must breathe. Under every exhale you must utter silently, in your mind, "Guidance."

JACK
How long must I do this for?

MONK
Until you have achieved guidance.

Scene III

to the audience in Anna's room

JACK

The guidance meditation lasted 18 months and three Buddhist temples later, I was back in college. I was dating this girl who was into poetry. She would, on what was becoming a regular basis, freak out, and say she wanted to visit a Buddhist temple and learn meditation.

ANNA

I just want to leave this place and become a Buddhist.

JACK

I tried that already. Can't I help you?

ANNA

What are you going to do that will help me? I need to leave this God forsaken place and get some guidance.

JACK

Let me guide you. I can teach you conscious breathing.

grabs two pillows from the bed to sit on the floor with

JACK

Keep your back straight. Close your eyes. Clear your head. Focus on the exhale of breath out your nostrils. For beginners, you can put two fingers up to your nose to feel the breath on them.

ANNA

It feels like I'm smelling my fingers.

JACK

Focus on the exhale!

ANNA

Okay!

after a few more breaths Jack pulls her fingers away from her mouth and kisses her; they kiss for another moment then stop abruptely

ANNA

That really helped calm me down. I'm not stressed anymore.

JACK

I know. It works pretty well.

ANNA

So what are you doing now that you are back in college?

JACK

Like what classes am I taking?

ANNA

Like are you religious or spiritual?

JACK

At present, I go on questioning Christianity. There are other religions I have come to share a connection with. One is Hinduism. After reading the Bhagavad-Gita, I came to understand a more personal God than as previously before in the Upanishads. Daoism catches my attention too. To meditate on the

Dao should be a rule for every person to try at least once in their life. I still connect with my meditation exercises, but have more or less abandoned the search amongst the Eastern religions. They do not fit into the equation.

ANNA

What equation?

JACK

You know in Calculus you hear the question asked a million times, (sarcastically) "What's the derivative?"

ANNA

What is the derivative?

JACK

I'm trying to solve for it.

ANNA

Maybe I can help you.

they kiss and climb into bed together; Jack climbs out of bed to address the audience

JACK

She didn't help. I didn't want her to know this, but I have no friends. Every man I know turns his back on me. I was in the woods the other day, and a deer walks by me. He was uneasy around me. I felt his frozen stare, as our hearts both leaped out of our chests in anxiety. Maybe I got it all backwards. That everything is pluses and minuses, like the negative charge of the bottom of a cloud and the building with the positive charge that meet somewhere in the air causing a lightning bolt. We forget the lightning. Are we grounded in a moment for the shocking truths which upon striking shall echo throughout mankind?

Scene IV

Anna sits at the table; enter Jack unpacking groceries

ANNA

Did you get the cheese?

JACK

For the mouse traps?

ANNA

For the wine and cheese party.

JACK

We lure them in with the cheese, then we poison them.

ANNA

More like we poison them, then offer them mold.

JACK

Cheese is right here.

sets cheese on the table

ANNA

Do you want to cut the cheese?

JACK

I would like to, but I went to the w.c. at Macy's.

ANNA

High class. Now grab a knife.

he grabs the salami and arranges it on a plate

JACK

I'll leave it up to the guests to cut their own cheese.

ANNA

You got the salami too.

JACK

I'm arranging it on the plate as we speak.

ANNA

You like playing with your salami don't you?

JACK

I set myself up for that one.

quits arranging the salami

ANNA

Come on. You're not done yet.

catches his passing body with an arm; they embrace

ANNA

Mind if I finish up on your salami?

JACK

Be my guest.

exit Jack; Anna arranges salami on the plate

<u>Scene V</u>

Anna, Jack, and Jennifer sip wine as Mark cuts the

cheese.

ANNA

Jack, Mark is studying to be a priest.

JACK

And how do you like the semanary?

JENNIFER

It's seminary.

JACK

That's what I said, 'semanary.' How do you like the semanary?

MARK

Greeks a bitch!

JENNIFER

Mark!

JACK

Does that mean you don't get in to heaven now since you simply did not let your yes be yes and your no be no?

MARK

No, I just have to recite a few extra Hail Mary's. Plus, I know the guy who runs confession.

JACK

That's funny, because I know the guy who knows the guy.

ANNA

Jesus Christ!

JENNIFER

Do not take the Lord's name in vain.

MARK

Loosen up a bit. You know, drink some more wine.

ANNA

Take some more communion.

JACK

I...I don't know if that joke is in good taste among Semanary Dude and Jennifer because of the whole trans-

ANNA

Trans-substantiation. Yeah, I'm Catholic too.

JACK

Okay good, so I'm not the only one who thinks we are vampires.

JENNIFER

Vampire stories have a lot of religious symbolism, more so than one would expect.

ANNA

Drink the blood and live forever. Cheers!

Jennifer gets sick; exit girls

MARK

Anna tells me you are working on an equation to solve life.

JACK

Isn't that what you are doing becoming a semanarian?

MARK

Have you ever considered becoming a priest?

JACK

Me? Take a vow of celibacy? Take a vow of celibacy? That has got to be hard for you.

MARK

Actually, the seminary-

JACK

Semanary.

MARK

Right, the seminary encourages us to date women as a test to see if we are truly prepared to do the LORD'S work.

JACK

How prepared are you?

MARK

I struggle with the question every day. Jennifer and I have been dating for a while now. We are at the point where we want to either set a date, or halt all relationship advancements.

JACK

Set a date...for the wedding!

MARK

I have been praying about this for some time now. She is such a beautiful woman, and I need God to tell me if he called us to his service, or if he wants me to marry and serve him in another way.

JACK

There has got to be another solution...

ACT II

Scene I

Jack imagines what Anna and Mark are saying about him and Jennifer.

ANNA

Hi, how are you doing.

MARK

Hey, how are you.

they embrace

ANNA

How is she?

MARK

She is with your man talking about us.

ANNA

Should we stay out extra late to make them worry?

MARK

They are already worried.

ANNA

Aren't you worried?

MARK

I think if we go back late, we can see who worries the most.

ANNA

I like that.

Exit Mark and Anna; enter Jack and Jennifer

JACK

This is the conversation that they

were having in my head.

JENNIFER
Seminary Boy and I are having problems.

JACK
Is that why Anna is comforting him?

JENNIFER
That's another thing. She needs to quit nosing around in everybody's problems and mind her own business.

JACK
She really is a nice girl though, but I can see why you would put that on her.

JENNIFER
And why are they together right now? Why is he talking to her about his problems instead of me?

JACK
Anna is not prepared for what she is in for.

JENNIFER
Same for Mark.

JACK
They need to understand that there are repercussions for their actions.

JENNIFER
I move to breakup.

JACK
I second that.

Scene II

Enter Mark and Jennifer

JENNIFER
So, how was your talk with Anna?

MARK
She is an understanding person.

JENNIFER
I guess I'm not understanding then.

MARK
No, you're different. I can't just confront you with all my problems and expect you to not be affected by them.

JENNIFER
You know I am here to listen, whatever you have to say.

MARK
But she is different. She is that friend that is there for me.

JENNIFER
I would rather you have a male best friend.

MARK
You can't handle us hanging out can you?

JENNIFER
No, and neither can Jack. This all has to stop before someone gets hurt.

MARK
So that's it, it's goodbye forever.

JENNIFER
We can still be friends.

MARK

Anna and I are friends.

JENNIFER

And we're not?

MARK

We are more than friends. We were boyfriend, girlfriend.

JENNIFER

I just have way too many trust issues with you. So now the burden has been lifted, you are free to become a priest.

exit Jennifer and Mark; enter Jack and Anna to eat breakfast at the table

ANNA

I made your favorite, bagel and peanut butter.

Jack purposely gets some peanut butter on his cheek

ANNA

You have some-

JACK

Right here?

ANNA

Right there.

JACK

Did I get it?

ANNA

Here let me...

She licks the peanut butter off his cheek as they turn breakfast into a make out session.

JACK

The last time I had this much fun with food, I was eating chocolate covered strawberries and having sex.

ANNA

That won't happen with me.

JACK

Why not?

ANNA

I'm a good girl.

JACK

You are not. You're actually a very naughty girl who needs to be punished.

ANNA

Stop. You know I'm saving myself for marriage.

JACK

You don't get it. I mean you're naughty because you were hanging out with Mark late.

ANNA

Yeah, just talking.

JACK

Okay.

ANNA

And I suppose you and Jennifer were just talking too?

JACK

I know we were just talking because we were talking about you and Mark.

ANNA

Gosh get over it.

JACK

We were talking about how you have to be friends with everybody. About how you have to get everyone to like you then you can be happy with yourself for being a good person. But Catholic guilt, oh that guilt, makes you feel like you are a horrible person, at least on the inside, 'cause it's what's on the inside that counts, huh?

ANNA

How dare you!

JACK

You two were cheating on us, huh?

ANNA

No, we were...

JACK

Why were you out so late, then?

ANNA

Mark was telling me about how he wants to become a priest, and yet how much he loves Jennifer.

JACK

Too bad she ended it too.

ANNA

Too? What the hell does that mean? Did you two make a pact?

JACK

We both decided you two were not worth it. The pain, no matter how innocent, still stings.

ANNA

First off, we didn't cheat. Second, why can't you just trust me?

JACK

I want to trust you; I just will never know because you have to move out now.

ANNA

Thanks for letting me lick peanut butter off you. How long were you waiting to break up with me?

to the audience

JACK

My relationship could be graphed on a Texas Instruments calculator to a point in my youth. They filled stories that dealt with the loss of friendship. Maybe I built up this defense mechanism that would allow me to commit to relationships without necessarily offering up a piece of myself. Maybe I didn't trust God. Maybe I didn't trust my own instincts.

Scene III

MARK

How can I tell if it was just a fling. You have gone away, I'm left adjusting. Emotions floated high, like the thoughts in our mind. You are the only girl, I ever hoped to find. How did I know you leaving created such a fuss. Those dangling conversations, you might care to discuss. Confusion is abundant. I don't know about you, feeling like the only one who doesn't know what to do. Now that you are gone, I have something to prove. Already waited to long, for you to make your move. A painful reality sears me like a burn. I wait until the day when you shall return.

putting on dress/makeup

ANNA

My humor will be cast into a cage, locked away, taking at least a year to recover. It has just regained its vigor, from my last imprisonment, to which I laugh to forget, each laugh less sincere than the last, harsher, more emotional; I cannot forget these scars so I mask them, dress them up, put on a costume and add makeup the foundation of a clown.

Mark chokes himself with a rosary

MARK

A necklace tugs at my throat. I can still breath, but with every inhale my throat pulls up a heavy heart, with every exhale my heart drops like a rock. It sits between breaths, like a lump in my throat that cannot be swallowed. It is on the stutter between inhaling again that it's full weight is felt. That last breath is out, and the tide is soon returning. It is starting to make the necklace taught, but even that instant is too late. It is the empty part of a breath. It is when neither the lungs nor the nose is operating. It is that last exhale of breath. No, it is the instant after I have breathed out the last exhale of breath. It is nothingness. It is despair. It is beneath my rib cage, it is my heart. It is my heart sinking like a rock, a heavy rock that burns in my throat when I exhale and tugs on the necklace when I inhale. It is pain. It is misery. It is knowledge. It is love, the love that is being choked to death out of all of us.

he dies

Scene IV

at the funeral, they walk by the open casket

JACK
He looks so white.

JENNIFER
Like a ghost.

ANNA
Makeup artists make it all look pretty for the cameras: blush, foundation, and mascara. Underneath it all we agree to appreciate the fake. Someone will do my makeup before I die; my face will be exposed in a casket, a perfect metaphor for the life I have led.

they take their seats

PRIEST
To live life one must overcome those which cannot be overcame,

love in it's beginnings and closings, time in the ruthless period of separation, and separation which wields the sword of pain. Life cannot rid of these it can only forget, for when new memories are birthed, old ones are buried.

MARK'S DAD

The solution is that there are no solutions. One universe after another, time is the grasping of eternity, the breaking up of the centuries, scores. Analyzing patterns of random, you are the news, the journalism of the day. You are living, currently breathing, blinking every second with this sense of eternity and searching for it. Mark was constantly searching for this, I know that he is in heaven, looking down upon us with a smile. You will be missed.

JACK

(mutters under breath)

Semanary Dude was a seven percenter?

JENNIFER

Was there anything I could have done to prevent Mark from killing himself?

ANNA

I keep getting this feeling that if I would not have had my conversation with him, then you two would still be together, and none of this mess would have happened.

JENNIFER
You cannot put that on yourself.

MARK'S DAD
Jack, Mark wanted you to have this.

hands him a composition journal

JACK
Thank you, I do not know what to say.

MARK'S DAD
There is nothing to say.

they hug

ACT III

Scene I

Jack sits in front of a fireplace, opens the journal

MARK
The moral fallacy, to start out by presupposing, "If this is true, then..." is like correcting a math problem, realizing that one number at the beginning subsequently flawed the answer to come out of it. To go back and rework the beginning is the intention. Plug it into a working formula. The variables are love and death.

LOVE
What in life is experience? What are its affects? Of the affects of experience, what does one truly feel?

MARK
Do not be fooled by the first question posed, for in life lies love and death, for in experience lies love and death. Therefore, life and experience hold the same value: in love and death.

LOVE
The affects are love and death. From experience one gathers opinion. This opinion, at least in the question of morality, Divides emotions. Was there a base experience?

DEATH
An avalanche that echoed throughout eternity. Perhaps a

salty undertow dragged out to sea, or to what heights did the soul traverse? A heavenly hike on snow covered dormant volcanoes; a baptismal dip in unsalted emerald waters the temperature of redemption.

MARK

The feeling of the affects, asks for one more layer to be removed. Love and death nakedly exposed. The adjectives being the affects, living implies a rhythm, a time of good and bad, a high and low, a base and a lofty. Love and death become adverbs in effect: The characterization of love is painted nude with candles as light; a softer hue for romantic beauty...

DEATH

Terror transformed as love: a sexually charged love the basest in nature which loses itself when acting out through lost memories, repeating heaven and hell in various ritualistic vices seeking to forget the haunting memory. Reflections are horrors, unchangeable ghosts. The future is transpiring; hope is dead.

MARK

The simplified question, "What in love and death is love and death?" Begs for the character of love and death to be oversimplified. The character of death as adverb is synonymous with love. The soul caught in the resurrection and redemption.

LOVE

An adolescent Christianity like the Gospel of Mark best represents the current attitude; the parable of the sower before the century late addition of the resurrection. Pale compared to the decade of development of Matthew, lacking the inclusiveness of Luke, seeking the prose of John.

DEATH

Best characterized as a grace or terror of the memory. The pantheon of moral grace and terror is the start of eschatology.

LOVE

One never feels life. One does not remember the moment of conception, the birth, or actually 'feel' living. It is like a heart beat. It is a heart beat—one could feel life only if it is lost, and of course one would not be feeling life but the loss of life, death.

JACK

Plugging in the variables, the problem reads, "One never feels love and death. One does not remember the moment of conception, the birth, or actually 'feel' love and death. It is like a heart beat.
It is a heart beat—one could feel love and death only if it is lost, and of course one would not be feeling love and death but the loss of love and death, death."

MARK

Simplification of the equation, the synonymous love for death, gives death a pulse, 'One could feel love only if it is lost,' but the loss of love is moral terror. Love becomes a neutralizing factor of death: death humbled is love if love is enough to humble oneself. Life becomes a painful dichotomy, a striving heaven-bound or hellbent mission.

LOVE

Love becomes the moral positive.

DEATH

Death becomes the moral negative. Therefore, death is the lone emotion of the affect of death as experience.

LOVE

Love is the lone emotion of the affect of love as experience.

DEATH

Those obsessed with love have the fear of death as a humbling factor resulting in death humbled as terror: it wears the mask of death itself as an ends to love and seeks eschatology through love manifest by grace as a means to avoid moral terror. Thus, a reason those that do not love are believed to not have a positive afterlife.

LOVE

One must have hope by correcting the past: God's judgment is moral terror, fear of the LORD.

MARK

What is sacred reflects the eternal. The splendor of hope through love is glorified in the morality of the reflection of the eternal.

LOVE

"Q" "E" "D".

DEATH

Quite excellently done.

the light from Jack's world fades; he jumps up as the light floods in

JACK

I feel my heart is racing. I am alive, but the world is no longer breathing. It crumbles beneath the reflections of a familiar face.

a knock at the door

JACK

There is strange world which knocks on the door. It has no right to knock, yet I feel an insistence on answering. Who is this stranger? It is another world calling, a beast upon the steps of light. Do I answer the call? She is an ashy white being not totally alive, but I am certain she is not dead.

opens door

DEATH

Guilt hangs around your neck. You

cannot cast it off. The poison from which this is producing is certain to bring about circumstantial change for the worst. That is why you have been summoned. The Negative Infinity, wish to meet with you in your decay. The people of Infinity may look down on us as leprous, infesting disease unnecessarily on the innocent, but it is the innocent which we must protect. Therefore it is the prideful which have been banished from our colony. They move about as if in a herd. We, The Negative Infinity, cordially invite you to a life of freedom, but you may not be free from growing anxiety and terror. Please accept our wishes.

hands Jack a note

JACK

How did you know I was in decay?

DEATH

We are all in decay.

JACK

This note is an answer to my cries.

shuts the door; tosses the note on the table; falls asleep; another knock

JACK

She came as if sent for no special purpose. The likes of being at my door no different than her being at the next. I could see she had good posture and well groomed ways. Her face read no different than the note in her small hands. It was indifferent, generic. Her knock on the door was yet another world calling.

LOVE

We, the The Infinity, summon you. You have been called to a life of wholeness and morality. You must go about your dealings without causing harm to others. You are invited to join the herd and as a result will enjoy much freedom. You will find your pride restored, your guilt diminished, and no more struggles with anxiety. We, The People of Infinity, see you and know what is troubling you. We extend our helping arms in return for a moral life and prideful being. We value human existence more than anyone else, especially more than those in The Negative Infinity. Please accept this note wholeheartedly.

hands Jack a note

JACK

What do you know of human existence?

shuts the door; tosses the note on the table next to the other one; decides to read the notes; enter Love and Death through the door

DEATH

It seems now that in the west humans have grown through science and self-discovery, through Darwin and Eliot.

LOVE

We look back and trace our steps: through time and space, through learning and repetition, through the worship of deities like the sun and moon, through the worship of the unknown personalities of wind and war, sea and rain, temple and human...

DEATH

The hunter-gatherer to the agricultural age, from the industrialization of food to the buildup of cities to kingdoms and empires...

LOVE

Creating the first law's value and the first coin's worth.

DEATH

Enmity of class status and enemy nations. Where have humans gone astray?

LOVE

We have forgotten our past. We have made a key and lock and thrown the key away. Future generations are puzzled by it.

DEATH

Now is the time to rise up, to fully grasp what is in store.

LOVE

In this heaven minds assign their own values to each action after objects are reassigned. This could be the past: a tragic incident holding on to previous memory or action. A set of core values need to be created that start with the choosing of actions. The mind works limitless, beyond the borders of rationality, a freedom and clarity of movement is found, where thoughts flow free in actions created by the mind.

DEATH

Hell is the death of thought: the action that loses its meaning, that has always meant the same. The art of being human is to move beyond this heaven and hell into making life more than just the positive or negative decision. The moral values that one has learned since infancy. They must be shaken up and shattered. A new meaning of life awaits those who seek it. You can set your own rules now.

JACK

Am I truly free? Two notes dangle in my mind. I must decide between "X" and "Y". I feel a strange attraction to "X", but "Y" is refreshing. My future lies in a simple decision. Each choice cuts at my being as I try to whittle away the mundane from the real, but it cannot be that easy. After all, no one disturbs my life now. I am a starving man who preys on the passerby, who sits in the background to watch reality unfold, receiving from the happenings which evolve around me, the unaffected. I have already made my decision. My life is a black hole which feeds on others, and so the notes prove worthless.

he burns the letters

Scene II

JACK

The God everyone tells you is some distant holy object to be worshiped is waiting for you.

ANNA

You see that is the way I was raised, that God is some glamorous, Ziegfeld follies production.

JACK

God wants to have a relationship with you, and like any functioning relationship, it
needs communication.

ANNA

How can you tell he is listening if he does not speak to you?

JACK

He speaks in quiet whispers.

ANNA

So he is your conscience like Disney?

JACK

Like Disney?

ANNA

"And always let your conscience be your guide."

JACK

No, he is something more. Like Big Brother to a paranoid schizophrenic. He's always listening.

ANNA

God has been so distant from me in my Catholic faith.

JACK

You know how in a relationship between two people who have been married for years, they do not have to communicate with each other all the time to know what they are feeling.

ANNA

God is that feeling?

JACK

God is the father I never had. He and I have spoken, not always on a daily basis, but he has waited patiently for that conversation to happen. He waits patiently for yours too.

ANNA

I think I am a protestant.

JACK

Heaven passed away with Mark.

lights cigarette

ANNA

It cannot be that bad.

JACK

There is only one meaning to my life now, and it is in jeopardy. Everything I have ever hoped for has been broken by reality. The infinite to which I once held on to so dearly is fleeting.

ANNA

How is this so? How can you lose

faith in the infinite?

JACK

By brutal denial, and the knowledge experienced on this earth. It is a knowledge that eats away at my future. To know the infinite and be fashioned in it since birth pains me. For I am now at a fuller understanding of life. To doubt the infinite is no easy task. You must be as passionate as those that believe in the infinite in order to doubt it. To fall short of this passion is to be lost in a paradox. You might say, "To know the infinite is false."

echos as it turns to thunder and lightning

JACK

One must then come to terms with the finite, but to not be able to grasp this is completely possible. If you cannot grasp the finite, you fall into despair or to embrace the infinite which has been determined as false.

ANNA

You solved the equation?

JACK

Everything comes down to pluses and minuses. I swear, Benjamin Franklin was five lightning rods short of declaring God dead.

his world fades as he crashes to the ground

ANNA

Jack, are you okay? Jack!

JACK

Yeah, I just need a glass of water or something.

ANNA

Did you just faint?

JACK

That would happen.

ANNA

I think you stood up to fast.

JACK

I would be the one to lose consciousness the moment I declare God dead.

ANNA

You are sweating profusely.

JACK

I'm okay. I'm fine.

ANNA

You sure?

JACK

No I'm ashamed of myself. Of course I'm good.

ANNA

What can I do to make it better?

JACK

You don't have to do that.

ANNA

Seriously. What can I do?

JACK

Whenever that happens to me I like

a good glass of cold milk and a game of chess.

ANNA

How about I get you the milk.

JACK

You asked me what you could do to make it better.

ANNA

If you asked me to jump off a bridge; I'm not going to jump off a bridge.

JACK

What if it was to show me your everlasting love?

ANNA

Only if we jumped together.

JACK

And the bridge was on a playground.

ANNA

And there was a mattress of wood chips on the ground.

JACK

Why did I ever break up with you?

MARK (VOICE)

You used Jennifer breaking up with me as an excuse to break up with Anna.

ANNA

You did not think I was faithful.

hits timer on the chess clock; they exchange lines with moves, each time striking the clock for emphasis

JACK

Faith has nothing to do with it.

ANNA

Is that all your precious math bullshit has to say?

JACK

If only life were a game of chess.

ANNA

If only I did not suck so bad at chess.

JACK

If only I were not so good at chess.

ANNA

How's that glass of milk?

JACK

Chess as a way to tell the future.

ANNA

Maybe it will, in the future.

JACK

The milk's great.

ANNA

I'm losing pretty badly.

JACK

I'll try to be quick and painless.

ANNA

Runaway.

JACK

Checkmate.

ANNA

You must be feeling better.

JACK

Thanks for stopping by.

ANNA

Jack ready for sleep?

JACK

Jack sleepy.

ANNA

Alright, I'll talk to you later.

JACK

Later.

turns around to Mark sitting at the chess board;

MARK

What if chess was the answer to life?

JACK

What if me playing you now was the answer to life?

MARK

Your move.

hits timer on the chess clock; they exchange lines with moves, each time striking the clock for emphasis

JACK

Would you rather have Anna or Jennifer?

MARK

Anna, no question.

JACK

Then why kill yourself?

MARK

I'm not a cheat.

JACK

Boy, you semanary boys take your sin seriously.

MARK

Are you going to move in on Jennifer now?

JACK

The thought crossed my mind.

Scene III

JENNIFER

I think we need to keep an eye on Jack.

ANNA

Now that Mark is gone...I agree.

JENNIFER

Has he said anything about what Mark's Dad gave him?

ANNA

You know that equation?

JENNIFER

Um.

ANNA

Think world religions plus calculus.

JENNIFER

Okay.

ANNA

He said that Mark had given him some sort of proof. He was

talking like he was high up in the clouds.

JENNIFER
Does he have high anxiety?

ANNA
Doesn't everybody?

JENNIFER
As long as he isn't depressed, I'm okay with it.

ANNA
But I think he may be missing a few marbles.

JENNIFER
As opposed to the marbles he has not lost?

ANNA
Like Mark took a few marbles.

JENNIFER
You probably took a few marbles.

ANNA
I can't get close to him anymore.

JENNIFER
You are too good for him.

ANNA
That's why I want you to be there for him.

JENNIFER
Why do I get all the responsibility?

ANNA
He's isolating. I don't like it. You need to go check up on him.

SCENE IV

MARK

Here, why don't you expand your mind.

hands him the notebook

JACK

Don't you think I've done enough expanding for one day?

MARK

To expand is to break down and become new.

JACK

Geez, expanding is a lot like recycling.

MARK

Our thoughts are like rain. They pour out down to earth, but eventually return to the sky to once again be poured out.

LOVE

Proof one: find the path to heaven.

DEATH

What was your path from the moment of conception?

MARK

If you plug your ears and listen, you may remember the human inside.

knock at the door; enter Jennifer

JACK

Burst through the door.

JENNIFER

I'm hear to hijack you.

JACK
Don't say that.

JENNIFER
Why?

JACK
Reminds me of those old movies where the crew mutinies the captain.

JENNIFER
I'm here to kill you.

JACK
Please, do it quick before Mark does.

JENNIFER
Is he making any sense?

JACK
He's developed a theorem with proofs and all.

JENNIFER
Did you show Anna?

JACK
No.

JENNIFER
Can I see it?

JACK
Do you think you are special or something?

JENNIFER
Jack, you know I loved him.

JACK
Why couldn't you stop him from

killing himself? Did you guys even talk?

JENNIFER
When we were together he felt like he was in a movie, everything had to be dealt with on the surface.

JACK
When did the dream become real for him?

JENNIFER
When it was already too late.

JACK
Some people are beyond help.

JENNIFER
I will never give up on people believing in themselves, which is why I believe in you.

JACK
What have I done to deserve this reward? You just want to look at the notebook.

JENNIFER
Pretty please. I'll have sex with you.

JACK
You have got to be joking.

JENNIFER
I wish I was.

they kiss

MARK
It's raining down roses with thorns in my side. I tried and I tried, but it was a failure.

LOVE
You leave nothing but whispers of afterthoughts as I trace shapes in sands that are blown in the wind.

MARK
Show me your pity, I'll show you my city. It's getting cold, down here where it's dark. Do not let me find my peace. Do not let me find my clarity.

LOVE
You're on the back of my camera. You are standing in the picture. Stills and photographs let you be frozen in time.

MARK
Surfing the highs of life, you find me again and again and again, and there has been one long low now, so low.

LOVE
You've let me fall to the ground. No where to fall from here. You've let me take my fall. You've let me fall to rock bottom.

Love and Mark get into bed with Jennifer and Jack

JACK
Ahhh!

JENNIFER
What is it?

JACK
Something cold.

JENNIFER
Was it my feet?

JACK

No. Something other worldy and cold.

JENNIFER

You don't believe in ghosts do you?

JACK

Chills were just sent through my body. You know a thought occurred to me, having sex with you is like me having sex with a dead guy.

JENNIFER

I never had sex with Mark.

JACK

Maybe you're the ice queen and your going to turn me to stone.

JENNIFER

The things you say-come on, let's get some sleep.

JACK

I can't sleep.

JENNIFER

Why not?

JACK

I don't know. I lay my head on the pillow, then Mark starts talking about Calculus.

JENNIFER

Maybe the subject will lull you to sleep.

JACK

I wish. My mind starts flying a hundred miles an hour. I'm wide awake.

JENNIFER
Does this happen often?

JACK
Only on nights I'm too sober to sleep. The worst part about it is that I've started to scribble my late night thoughts into a journal. And the results, boy if I could tell you the results.

JENNIFER
Let me guess. You can't read your own handwriting.

JACK
Yes or worse: I can read it, but it doesn't make any sense to a sane person so I crumble up the paper and throw it away.

JENNIFER
Have you ever been tested?

JACK
I think one time God tested me.

JENNIFER
No, I mean for chemical dependency.

JACK
I uh-

JENNIFER
You seem so up and down these days.

JACK
Isn't life up and down?

JENNIFER
Yes it is, but there is a constant that needs to be maintained.

JACK
Constant. That's good. Mind if I use that for my formula?

JENNIFER
I don't care. As long as you let me get help.

JACK
You seem to be helping me quite nicely.

JENNIFER
Come on! You talk about leaving for a few days, "getting lost." I know a crisis residence where you can chill out for a few days maybe get some sleep.

JACK
Sleep is good.

JENNIFER
You have no idea how sleep can affect your mental health, same with putting in long hours of work or over scheduling, the body can do so much, but you start to wear yourself thin, too much stress, burning the candle on both ends. You know all the cliches.

JACK
This crisis residence doesn't happen to be in a desert?

JENNIFER
No. No drugs. Just a mini vacation of sobriety and sunshine.

JACK
Wouldn't hurt me, I guess.

JENNIFER

Then it's settled. In the morning, I'm taking you to the crisis residence.

JACK

I can't sleep. No bother waiting till morning.

JENNIFER

Let's go.

ACT IV

Scene I

crisis residence;
Counselor's office

COUNSELOR
So how are you, Mr. Jackson.

JACK
Call me Jack.

COUNSELOR
Your folder says Mr. Jackson. Shall I change it to Jack?

JACK
Please.

COUNSELOR
What brings you in here?

JACK
I've been struggling with a recent death of someone close to me.

COUNSELOR
Now, I just need to ask you a few more questions.

JACK
Okay.

COUNSELOR
Do you ever think about killing yourself?

JACK
No.

COUNSELOR
Do you have thoughts to harm yourself?

JACK

No. Why would I?

COUNSELOR

Do you hear voices telling you to do things?

JACK

No. Well, I've been hearing his voice.

COUNSELOR

The dead friend's?

JACK

Correct.

COUNSELOR

What's he saying?

JACK

He's telling me to join him.

COUNSELOR

Do you listen or ignore the voices.

JACK

I listen to them, then I ignore them.

COUNSELOR

Yeah, they tend to get a little repetitive don't they?

JACK

Only the shameful ones.

COUNSELOR

There is a book that I want you to read called *An Unquiet Mind: A Memoir of Moods and Madness.*

She hands him the book

COUNSELOR

We'll meet again.

Scene II

exit Jack to room where Sixties Hippie draws on a chalkboard

SIXTIES HIPPIE

Shit. Shit. Piece of ass. Worthless.

JACK

That describes tourette syndrome very nicely. You can't control. Imagine not being able to control what you are saying. It would be pretty bad.

SIXTIES HIPPIE

Talking, but with all of the energies flowing outward.

JACK

What you are saying is not flowing outward. You and I have contrasting realities.

SIXTIES HIPPIE

Ultimately, they form together into a single unity. They all become the same. The same as in one.

JACK

Dude, everything is mitosis.

SIXTIES HIPPIE

Why?

JACK

Because everything is copied over and over again a billion times.

SIXTIES HIPPIE

Are you, me, in a different point in time?

Sixties Hippie draws a center point and spirals in circles outwards. He draws the sun radiating with rays like hairs.

SIXTIES HIPPIE

Memories scattered throughout the suns rays.

JACK

Mathematics in time.

SIXTIES HIPPIE

This is everything. This is everything at creation at one point, starting here. Do you see the point? That is all things combined. Almost like a billion black holes emerging into one extremely compact, what you would describe as matter, and as Einstein showed us, matter is energy. Therefore, we are all just as one being, experiencing ourselves subjectively being created one person as itself and another and would see himself and would not recognize himself. So he is not seeing himself subjectively being created one person as itself, he sees himself but he would not recognize himself. So he has torrets, but maybe he doesn't have torrets, because he doesn't recognize himself.

JACK

Why would they go back to the one?

SIXTIES HIPPIE

To experience everything all over again.

JACK

Well, then they would just go back to the one every time.

SIXTIES HIPPIE

The universe expands outward, will come back around, and combine again.

JACK

I need to meet with the Counselor.

SIXTIES HIPPIE

The trees the leaves the deeds...Plant them for our dying needs.

Scene III

Jack enters Counselor's office

COUNSELOR

Be with you in one moment.

plays with his phone

COUNSELOR

How are you feeling?

JACK

I feel like I have the worst hangover in the world.

COUNSELOR

Keep taking the medicine, it should help.

grabs the composition journal; Jack cringes

COUNSELOR

Now, tell me if any of this sounds familiar...

(reads methodically and with a monotone voice)

We look back and trace our steps, through time and space, through learning and repetition, through the worship of deities like the sun and the moon, through the worship of the unknown personalities, of wind and war, sea and rain, temple and human.

JACK

Yeah, okay you can stop. I wrote that.

COUNSELOR

I asked you if it sounded familiar. I have no intention of stopping. You need to hear what you wrote to know the manic state you were in when this all happened.

JACK

I don't see what good this is going to do me.

COUNSELOR

(louder, more enunciated)

The hunter-gatherer to the agricultural age. From the industrialization of food to the buildup of cities, to kingdoms and empires. Creating the first law's value, the first coin's worth. Enmity of class status and enemy nations.

(reading to shame

Jack)

Where have humans gone astray? We have forgotten our past. We have made a key and lock and thrown the key away. Future generations are puzzled by it. Now is the time to rise up, to fully grasp what is in store.

JACK

I'm surprised you can read my handwriting.

COUNSELOR

Jack, what do you mean, to fully grasp what is in store?

JACK

As a child, I wanted one thing in life, to have my dark night of the soul.

COUNSELOR

So this is your cave experience.

JACK

I guess you could say that. It was as if I broke all the mental barriers down in my mind until I was free. I have been working on an equation of life.

COUNSELOR

Solving this equation was a way of freeing yourself?

JACK

You could imagine that.

COUNSELOR

We also found a grocery list of Bible verses: Matthew, Hebrews, James, Isaiah, John, Proverbs, Revelation, and Ecclesiastes.

JACK
Everything is meaningless.

COUNSELOR
Now Jack, how does, in your own words, one rise up and grasp what is in store, if according to this Bible verse, everything is meaningless?

JACK
I think you are missing the point.

COUNSELOR
Enlighten me.

JACK
Because the thing I am trying to grasp is how a sinner can get into heaven after having already fallen away.

COUNSELOR
Go on.

JACK
Like that night I came to a point where I had convinced myself that I could never again become a Christian again because I had already screwed up, to the point where it did not matter for me anymore because I had thrown out the ideas of heaven and hell and the infinite. Thus, the meaninglessness of it all.

COUNSELOR
Well, we have you on bipolar medication now, and if you want I can get a pastor to visit.

JACK
I would like that. Thank you.

they stand and shake hands

JACK

How long do you think I will have to be on meds for?

COUNSELOR

The rest of your life.

ACT V

Scene I

supper at the behavioral health clinic; Jack spots a pale white woman his age at a table and sits across from her; he reads his book

JACK
What brings you in here?

SUICIDAL GIRL
My family thinks I am suicidal.

JACK
Are you?

SUICIDAL GIRL
I just don't see any real reason for living the American dream anymore. My family put me in here because they were afraid of me and didn't know what to do with me. I'm into drugs, which they don't like, and I told them I'm not going to quit.

JACK
Sounds like they care about you.

SUICIDAL GIRL
My mom is the worst. We get into fights all the time. My dad just sits quietly behind what she says. I don't see any real reason as to why I'm even here. What about you, tell me why you are here.

JACK
Manic episode. Now they say I need to take meds the rest of my life because they think I am

bipolar.

SUICIDAL GIRL
That's not that bad. It's not like it's the end of the world or anything. I mean, mental health is a real issue that people struggle with. People who hear voices in their heads telling them to do things is real, although I try to think it is not.

NURSE
Jack, the Counselor would like to see you.

Scene II

Counselor's office

COUNSELOR
What did you think of the book?

JACK
I found the book to be captivating, a bit on the feminine side.

COUNSELOR
What did she have to say about living with bipolar?

JACK
She's too much into talking about her relationships. She doesn't really talk that much about how the disease has affected her.

COUNSELOR
So you didn't get anything out of the book?

JACK
Not really. Although I can relate

to some of the manic states she has been in. So there is one point that was good.

COUNSELOR

Okay. Yeah, tell me a little more about what she said.

JACK

She said that she felt like she had all the energy in the world; she wasn't sleeping.

COUNSELOR

Okay. Okay good. Good. So now you have something to look out for, like warning signs that will alert you when this may happen to you.

JACK

Yeah, I guess.

COUNSELOR

Well, we're out of time. That's it for today.

Jack exits; the door closes

<u>Scene III</u>

to the audience

JACK

For so long, not believing I was ill had led me time and time again to broken down emotional messes. Not until believing I had a problem...That's not the right word. Not until accepting that I had a problem. There, accepting, not until fully accepting every wrong, every word and thought in denial, can I take positive steps towards recovery. There is no miracle pill that can change my mind set on life. Positive steps away from denial must be adhered to, and no doctor, psychiatrist, or psychologist can help me if I cannot help myself. Illness must be accepted not only as an illness, but as a life altering illness. It requires that I change my outlook on life.

www.ingramcontent.com/pod-product-compliance
Ingram Content Group UK Ltd.
Pitfield, Milton Keynes, MK11 3LW, UK
UKHW041916190726
13854UKWH00003B/1275